THE BEST CHRISTMAS PRESENT IN THE WORLD

By Michael Morpurgo
Illustrated by Michael Foreman

EGMONT

We bring stories to life

First published in this edition in Great Britain 2004 by Egmont Books Limited
239 Kensington High Street, London W8 6SA

Text copyright © 2004 Michael Morpurgo
Illustrations copyright © 2004 Michael Foreman
Cover photo courtesy of the Imperial War Museum, London

The moral rights of the author and illustrator have been asserted

ISBN 1 4052 1518 6
3 5 7 9 10 8 6 4

A CIP catalogue record for this title is available from the British Library

Printed and bound in Singapore

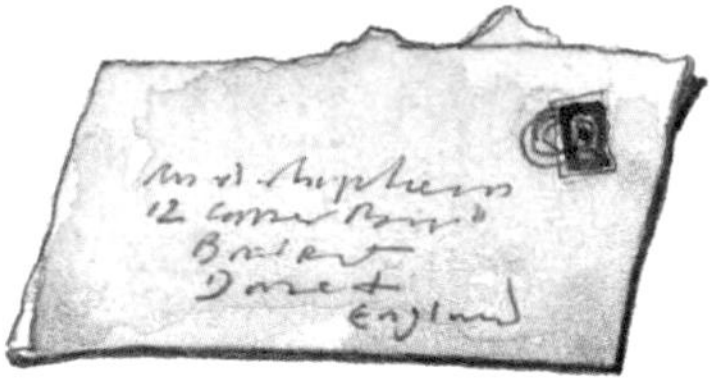
Dorset
England

To all those on both sides who
took part in the Christmas
truce of 1914.

I spotted it in a junk shop in Bridport, a roll-top desk. The man said it was early nineteenth century, and oak. I had been looking for a desk like this for years, but never found one I could afford. This one was in bad condition, the roll top in several pieces, one leg clumsily mended, scorch marks all down one side.

It was going for very little money, and I reckoned I was just about capable enough to have a go at restoring it. It would be a risk, a challenge, but here was my chance to have a roll-top desk at last. I paid the man and brought it back to my workroom at the back of the garage. I began work on it on Christmas Eve, mostly because the house was resonating with overexcited relatives and I wanted some peace and quiet.

I removed the roll top completely and pulled out the drawers. Each one of them confirmed that this would be a bigger job than I had first thought. The veneer had lifted almost everywhere – it looked like flood damage. Both fire and water had clearly taken their toll on this desk. The last draw was stuck fast. I tried all I could to ease it out gently. In the end I used brute force. I struck it sharply with the side of my fist and the drawer flew open to reveal a shallow space underneath, a secret drawer. There was something in there. I reached in and took out a small black tin box. Taped to the top of it was a piece of lined note paper, and written on it in shaky handwriting: 'Jim's last letter, received 25th January 1915. To be buried with me

when the time comes.'

I knew as I did it that it was wrong of me to open the box, but curiosity got the better of my scruples. It usually does.

Inside the box there was an envelope. The address read: 'Mrs Jim Macpherson, 12 Copper Beeches, Bridport, Dorset'. I took out the letter and unfolded it. It was written in pencil and dated at the top 26th December 1914.

Dearest Connie

I write to you in a much happier frame of mind because something wonderful has just happened that I must tell you about at once. We were all standing to in our trenches yesterday morning, Christmas morning. It was crisp and quiet all about, as beautiful a morning as I've ever seen, as cold and frosty as a Christmas morning should be.

I should like to be able to tell you that
we began it. But the truth, I'm ashamed to
say, is that Fritz began it. First someone
saw a white flag waving from the trenches
opposite. Then they were calling out to
us from across no-man's-land, 'Happy
Christmas, Tommy! Happy Christmas!'
When we had got over the surprise

some of us shouted back, 'Same to you, Fritz! Same to you!'

I thought that would be that. We all did. But then suddenly one of them was up there in his grey greatcoat and waving a white flag.

'Don't shoot, lads!' Someone shouted. And no one did. Then there was another

Fritz up on the parapet, and another.

'Keep your heads down,' I told the men. 'It's a trick.' But it wasn't.

One of the Germans was waving a bottle above his head. 'It is Christmas Day, Tommy. We have schnapps. We have sausage. We meet you? Yes?'

By this time there were dozens of them walking towards us across no-man's-land and not a rifle between them.

Little Private Morris was the first up.

'Come on, boys. What are we waiting for?'

And then there was no stopping them.

I was the officer. I should have called a halt

to it there and then, I suppose, but the

truth is that it never even ocurred to me.

All along their line and ours I could see

men walking slowly towards one another, grey coats, khaki coats meeting in the middle. And I was one of them. I was part of this. In the middle of the war we were making peace.

You cannot imagine, dearest Connie, my feelings as I looked into the eyes of the

Fritz officer who approached me, hand outstretched.

'Hans Wolf,' he said, gripping my hand warmly and holding it. 'I am from Dusseldorf. I play the cello in the orchestra. Happy Christmas.'

'Captain Jim Macpherson,' I replied. 'And a happy Christmas to you too. I'm a school teacher from Dorset, in the west of England.'

'Ah, Dorset,' he smiled. 'I know this

place. I know it very well.'

We shared my rum ration and his excellent sausage. And we talked, Connie, how we talked. He spoke almost perfect English. But it turned out that he had never set foot in Dorset. He had learned all he knew of England from school, and from reading books in English. His favourite writer was Thomas Hardy, his favourite book *Far from the Madding Crowd*. So out there in no-man's-land we

talked of Bathsheba and
Gabriel Oak and
Sergeant Troy and Dorset.
He had a wife and one son,
born just six months ago. As I
looked about me there were huddles
of khaki and grey everywhere, all over
no-man's-land, smoking, laughing, talking,
drinking, eating. Hans Wolf and I shared
what was left of your wonderful Christmas
cake, Connie. He thought the marzipan

was the best he had ever tasted. I agreed. We agreed about everything Connie, and he was my enemy. There never was a Christmas party like it, Connie.

Then someone, I don't know who, brought out a football. Greatcoats were dumped in piles to make goal posts, and the next thing we knew it was Tommy against Fritz out in the middle of no-man's-land. Hans Wolf and I looked on and cheered, clapping our hands and stamping our feet,

to keep out the cold as much as anything.
There was a moment when I noticed our
breaths mingling in the air between us. He
saw it too and smiled.

'Jim Macpherson,' he said after a while, 'I
think this is how we should resolve this war.
A football match. No one dies in a football
match. No children are orphaned. No wives

become widows.'

'I'd prefer cricket,' I told him. 'Then we Tommies could be sure of winning, probably.' We laughed at that, and together we watched the game. Sad to say, Connie, Fritz won, two goals to one. But as Hans Wolf generously said, our goal was wider than theirs, so it wasn't quite fair.

The time came, and all too soon, when the game was finished, the schnapps and the cake and the rum and the sausage had long since run out, and we knew it was all over. I wished Hans well and told him I hoped he would see his family again soon, that the fighting would end and we could all go home.

'I think that is what every soldier wants,

on both sides,' Hans Wolf said. 'Take care, Jim Macpherson. I shall never forget this moment, nor you.'

He saluted and walked away from me slowly – unwillingly, I felt. He turned to wave just once and then became one of the hundreds of grey-coated men drifting back towards their trenches.

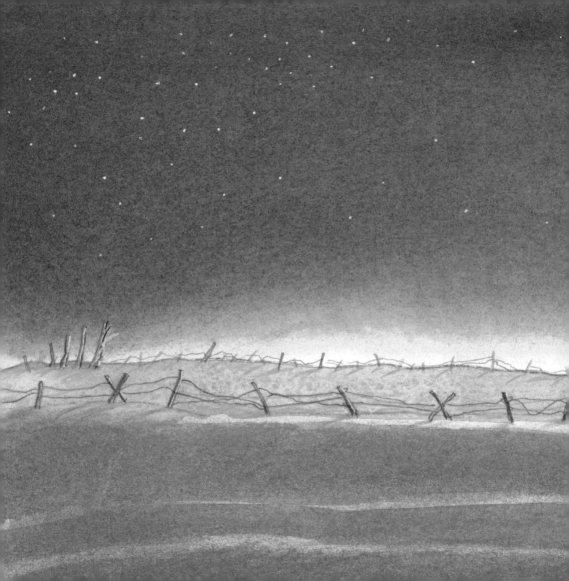

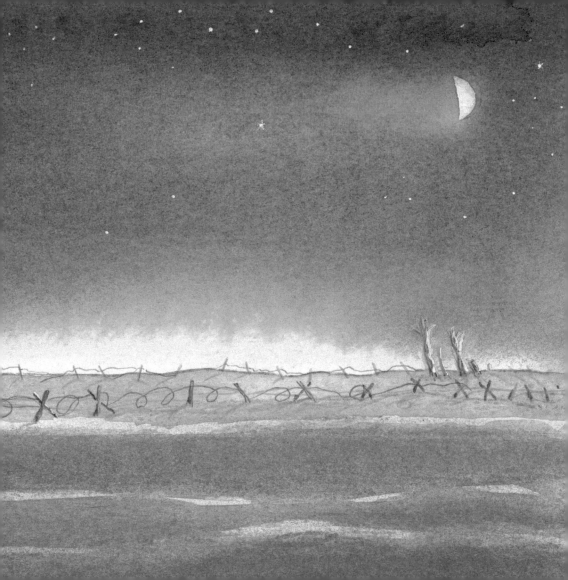

That night, back in our dugouts we heard them singing a carol, and singing it quite beautifully. It was 'Stille Nacht' – 'Silent Night'. Our boys gave them a rousing chorus of 'While shepherds watched.' We exchanged carols for a while and then we all fell silent. We had had our time of peace and goodwill, a time I will treasure as long as I live.

Dearest Connie, by Christmas time next year, this war will be nothing but a distant and terrible memory. I know from all that happened today how much both armies long for peace. We shall be together again soon, I'm sure of it.

Your loving Jim

I folded the letter again and slipped it carefully back into its envelope. I told no one about my find, but kept my shameful intrusion to myself. It was this guilt, I think, that kept me awake all night. By morning, I knew what I had to do. I made an excuse and did not go to church with the others. Instead I drove into Bridport, just a few miles away. I asked a boy walking his dog where Copper Beeches was.

Number twelve turned out to be nothing but a burnt-out shell, the roof gaping, the windows boarded up. I knocked at the house next door and asked if anyone knew the whereabouts of a Mrs Macpherson. Oh yes, said the old man in his slippers, he knew her well. A lovely old lady, he told me, a bit muddled-headed, but at her age she was entitled to be, wasn't she? 101 years old. She had been in the house when it caught fire. No one really knew how the fire had started, but it could well have been candles. She used candles rather than electricity, because she always thought electricity was too expensive. The fireman had got her out just in time. She was in a nursing home now, he told me, Burlington House, on the Dorchester road, on the other side of town.

I found Burlington House Nursing Home easily enough. There were paper

chains up in the hallway and a lighted
Christmas tree stood in the corner
with a lop-sided angel on top. I said
I was a friend come to visit Mrs
Macpherson to bring her a
Christmas present. I could
see through into the
dining room where
everyone was
wearing a
paper hat

and singing along to 'Good King Wenceslas'. The matron had a hat on too and seemed happy enough to see me. She even offered me a mince pie. She walked me along the corridor.

'Mrs Macpherson is not in with the others,' she told me. 'She's rather confused today so we thought it best if she had a good rest. She's no family you know – no one visits. So I'm sure she'll be only too pleased to see you.' She took me

into a conservatory with wicker chairs and potted plants all around and left me.

The old lady was sitting in a wheelchair, her hands folded in her lap. She had silver white hair pinned into a wispy bun. She was gazing out at the garden.

'Hello,' I said.

She turned and looked up at me vacantly.

'Happy Christmas, Connie,' I went on. 'I found this. I think it's yours.'

As I was speaking her eyes never left my face. I opened the tin box and gave it to her. That was the moment her eyes lit up with recognition and her face became suffused with a sudden glow of happiness. I explained about the desk, about how I had found it, but I don't think she was listening. For a while she said nothing, but stroked the letter tenderly with her fingertips.

Suddenly she reached out and took my

hand. Her eyes were filled with tears. 'You told me you'd come home by Christmas, dearest,' she said. 'And here you are, the best Christmas present in the world. Come closer, Jim dear, sit down.'

I sat down beside her, and she kissed my cheek. 'I read your letter so often, Jim, every day. I wanted to hear your voice in my head. It always made me feel you were with me. And now you are. Now you're

back you can read it to me yourself. Would you do that for me? I just want to hear your voice again, Jim. I'd love that so much. And then perhaps we'll have some tea. I've made you a nice Christmas cake, marzipan all around. I know how much you love marzipan.'